White Sox Coloring and Activity Book

1st Edition Collectible

By Sara A. Miller

WhiteSoxColoringBook.com

Hawk's Nest
Publishing, LLC

HawksNestPublishing.com

Official Licensee -- Major League Baseball Players Association
visit www.MLBPLAYERS.com, the Players Choice on the web.

Major League Baseball trademarks and copyrights are used with permission of
Major League Baseball Properties, Inc. MLB.com

ISBN-10: 0-9823903-0-0
ISBN-13: 978-0-9823903-0-6

Illustrations by
Scott Waddell
www.ScottWaddellFinearts.com

Cover Design and Interior Layout by
Matt Haas
www.MattHaas.com

*Special thanks to Kirby Sprouls, Dawson Cheney, Don and Kimberly Cheney, Jo Hershberger
and Evan Haas for their contributions to the White Sox Coloring and Activity Book.*

Jim Thome extends his bat and focuses on the pitcher in his daunting at-bat routine.

Carlos Quentin unleashes his power on an unsuspecting rookie pitcher.

U.S. Cellular Field offers the ultimate baseball experience for the whole family.

Use your knowledge about the *White Sox* to solve the following crossword puzzle.

Crossword Puzzle 1 - *White Sox* History

Across

2 The White Sox won 94 games in the _____ season of old Comiskey Park in 1990.

5 Jerry _____ and Eddie Einhorn purchased the White Sox from Bill Veeck's group in 1981.

7 The White Sox played in St. Paul, Minnesota, and were originally known as the _____ before moving to Chicago in 1900.

8 Rookie pitcher Charlie Robertson threw the only _____ game in White Sox history on April 30, 1922.

11 The Chicago White Sox _____ their first game against Milwaukee at 39th and Princeton in Chicago.

12 Luke _____ captured the American League batting title with an average of .388 and a 27-game hit streak in the same season.

15 On August 14, 1939, the White Sox played the first _____ game at Comiskey Park against the Browns.

17 In 1917, Chicago won its second _____ title, beating the New York Giants. (two words)

18 In 1977, the White Sox were nicknamed the "South Side _____" since nine players hit ten or more home runs that season.

19 Chicago plays its first official _____ League game in Chicago against Cleveland.

20 The first White Sox player to win an American League home run crown was Bill _____.

Down

1 _____ Joe Jackson's contract was purchased for $31,500 from Cleveland on August 20, 1915.

3 Luis Aparicio became the everyday _____ in 1956 over Chico Carrasquel.

4 Carlton _____ set a Major League record for home runs by a catcher on August 17, 1990.

6 The White Sox demolished _____ rows from the top of the upper deck, eliminating 6,600 seats following the 2003 season.

9 Charles _____ purchased the franchise in 1893.

10 The White Sox clinched the 1959 American League pennant in a game against the _____.

13 Chicago won its first game as the White Stockings against the University of Illinois in _____.

14 Minnie Minoso hit a _____ in his first at bat for Chicago. (two words)

16 The first MLB All-Star Game was played in _____ on July 6, 1933, as as part of the World's Fair.

Use your knowledge about the *White Sox* to solve the following crossword puzzle.

Crossword Puzzle 1 - *White Sox* History

Solution is on page 53.

Connect-the-Dots #1

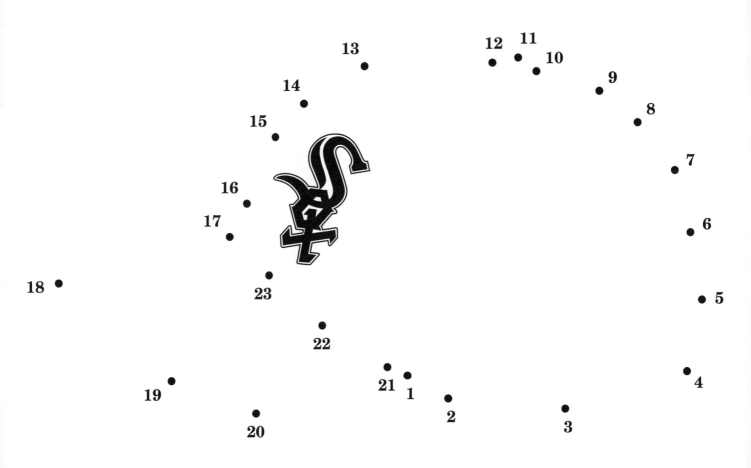

Worn by young and old, this is the sign of a true *White Sox* fan.

A.J. Pierzynski's strong arm threatens any runner trying to steal.

Left-handed starting pitcher John Danks is a mainstay in the *White Sox* rotation.

Word Search #1
White Sox Players

```
J S X Q U E N T I N F V K Y Y K E S N Q
D H T A M K B R H S E U L J M D Y E L J
Q D I O D W I R M O K B N J D Y M A Y V
L O H X A P Z Y B N R N B U E H R L E G
X T O O N K D E I U O N E R J R N B R T J
F E N B K Y M R R S C G T J O P O I V N
R L Y J S M B V R I U Y D O M A M L K B
K C O S R E V E K E M S T P N E D Z O M
H D K Y N V D S W S L A Z T T J C W Q C
C J Z I D N N O B I Z R R E N B P Z A H
M S L K A Y E E Y W Q E B D Z U I X U Y
C A Z G Z E G A O C O R L A D T G A C N
E P S R D L S D J Y N T Z C F G E Y H N
T Q E A Z U N X X F J N V W F T D G Z U
V I J Z Z V G S L F D O K O N E R K O J
P M Y H D C L W Q T W C Q O N Z E N N L
```

Try to find all the words contained in the list below: (Hint: Words may be found by looking up and down, across, or diagonally. Some words are even spelled backwards!)

ANDERSON	COLON	DYE	KONERKO	RAMIREZ
BETEMIT	CONTRERAS	FLOYD	LINEBRINK	THOME
BROADWAY	DANKS	GETZ	PIERZYNSKI	THORNTON
BUEHRLE	DOTEL	JENKS	QUENTIN	WISE

Solution is on page 53.

2009 *White Sox* Player Challenge
White Sox Roster effective March 19, 2009

No	PITCHERS	B	T	HT	WT	DOB
41	Lance Broadway	R	R	6-3	190	08/20/83
56	Mark Buehrle	L	L	6-2	230	03/23/79
53	D.J. Carrasco	R	R	6-3	220	04/12/77
40	Bartolo Colon	R	R	5-11	245	05/24/73
52	Jose Contreras	R	R	6-4	255	12/06/71
50	John Danks	L	L	6-1	200	04/15/85
26	Octavio Dotel	R	R	6-0	215	11/25/73
62	Jack Egbert	L	R	6-3	220	05/12/83
34	Gavin Floyd	R	R	6-5	230	01/27/83
45	Bobby Jenks	R	R	6-3	275	03/14/81
57	Kelvin Jimenez	R	R	6-2	195	10/27/80
71	Scott Linebrink	R	R	6-2	215	08/04/76
48	Jeffrey Marquez	R	R	6-2	190	08/10/84
54	Clayton Richard	L	L	6-5	240	09/12/83
46	Adam Russell	R	R	6-8	250	04/14/83
37	Matt Thornton	L	L	6-5	245	09/15/76
43	Ehren Wassermann	S	R	6-0	185	12/06/80
No	CATCHERS	B	T	HT	WT	DOB
12	A.J. Pierzynski	L	R	6-4	240	12/30/76
No	INFIELDERS	B	T	HT	WT	DOB
15	Wilson Betemit	S	R	6-3	230	11/02/81
22	Josh Fields	R	R	6-1	220	12/14/82
17	Chris Getz	L	R	6-0	185	08/30/83
14	Paul Konerko	R	R	6-2	220	03/05/76
18	Brent Lillibridge	R	R	5-11	190	09/18/83
5	Jayson Nix	R	R	5-11	185	08/26/82
10	Alexei Ramirez	R	R	6-3	185	09/22/81
No	OUTFIELDERS	B	T	HT	WT	DOB
32	Brian Anderson	R	R	6-2	220	03/11/82
23	Jermaine Dye	R	R	6-5	245	01/28/74
7	Jerry Owens	L	L	6-3	195	02/16/81
20	Carlos Quentin	R	R	6-2	220	08/28/82
31	DeWayne Wise	L	L	6-1	195	02/24/78
No	DESIGNATED HITTERS	B	T	HT	WT	DOB
25	Jim Thome	L	R	6-3	255	08/27/70

2009 *White Sox* Challenge

Use the names on the *White Sox* roster to fill in the correct players who made these accomplishments.

1. Acquired from the San Francisco Giants, White Sox catcher _____ typically finds himself at the center of memorable plays.

2. _____ certainly brings the heat as the White Sox closer. He's been clocked around 100 mph!

3. _____ hit home run number 541 in 2008, placing him 14th on the all-time home run leaderboard.

4. _____ had a blazing start in 2008, leading his team with 36 home runs.

5. Lefty _____ has a reputation for being one of the most efficient and accurate pitchers in the American League.

6. Acting captain _____ has been named to the All-Star team three of his nine years with the White Sox.

7. _____ sealed his position as a fan favorite by batting a strong .375 during the series against the Rays.

8. _____ pitched eight innings during the White Sox/Twins Central Division playoff game at the end of the season, allowing only 2 hits in a White Sox victory.

9. _____ set a Major League rookie record by hitting four grand slams during the 2008 season.

10. White Sox center fielder, _____, relinquished his previous number 44 to veteran catcher Toby Hall and now wears number 32 in honor of Magic Johnson.

11. _____ should be ready to chew up some innings this season after sitting out with a shoulder injury for a bit in 2008.

Solution is on page 54.

Use your knowledge about the *White Sox* to solve the following crossword puzzle.

Crossword Puzzle 2 - *White Sox* Fun Facts

Across

3 The fewest _____ ever recorded by a White Sox team in a single season came in 2002 with 97.

5 Curent Detroit Tigers rightfielder who got his start with the White Sox.

6 The number of White Sox players in 2006 who hit at least 30 homers in the same season – a White Sox first.

8 Jimmy Dykes _____ the White Sox for twelve seasons - the longest tenure in White Sox history.

12 The cornerstone of the original _____ Park was laid on St. Patrick's Day in 1910.

13 Doc White _____ 45 consecutive scoreless innings in 1904.

16 The World Series Champions, White Sox were dubbed the "_____ Wonders" in 1906, for their team batting average was .230.

17 _____ was signed as a free agent after 11 seasons with the Boston Red Sox. (two words)

18 _____ was the first White Sox player to win the American League MVP award in 1959.

Down

1 Gary _____ was voted the top rookie in the American League in 1963.

2 Only White Sox player named to the All Star team in 2007. (two words)

4 Robin Ventura hit two _____ versus Texas in 1995.

7 This infamous surgery typically performed on a pitcher was named after this 1968 White Sox All Star. (two words)

9 Jose Valentin is the only White Sox player to hit for the _____ cycle. He did it on April 27, 2000.

10 _____ is the White Sox Mascot.

11 Current White Sox manager named Rookie of the Year in 1985. (two words)

14 Frank _____ hit the first White Sox home run in the new Comiskey Park on August 22, 1991 - the first night game in the new park.

15 Chris Singleton became the first White Sox rookie to hit for the _____.

Use your knowledge about the *White Sox* to solve the following crossword puzzle.

Crossword Puzzle 2 - *White Sox* Fun Facts

Solution is on page 54.

A crouching Paul Konerko awaits the throw at first base.

Bobby Jenks prepares to deliver one of his signature screaming fastballs.

Jim Thome acknowledges the "Thome" chants from the crowd after hitting his 500th home run.

Ball or strike? Fair or Foul? Safe or Out? Usually, the umpires have to make the tough decisions, but now... YOU MAKE THE CALL!

Here's the situation...

It's the bottom of the 4th inning with one out in a divisional matchup between the Detroit Tigers and the Chicago White Sox. Alexei Ramirez is on first base with DH Jim Thome at the plate. Thome hits a fly ball to right field. Tigers outfielder Magglio Ordeñez makes the catch while on the run. Unable to stop his momentum, Ordoñez flips over the railing into the stands. Ramirez, after the ball is caught, tags up and makes it safely into third base.

What is the correct call?

Solution is on page 54.

Solve the *White Sox* Scramble

Unscramble the letters below to reveal *White Sox* words or phrases:

1. MEYKSCOI RKPA

   _____ ____

2. *Example:* KRANF STMOAH

   FRANK THOMAS

3. TOUSHPWA

   _____

4. FWRORSIEK

   _____

5. SLALM LBAL

   _____ ____

6. ZIEOZ LIUGNEL

   _____ _____

7. TOSUH DISE

   _____ ____

8. NACEMAIR EEGALU

   _____ _____

Solution is on page 55.

Alexei Ramirez exhibits his blazing speed on the bases.

White Sox Nicknames Challenge

Match these famous White Sox nicknames to the players (from the past and present) that appear on the next page:

"Burls"	"Black Jack"	"Moose"	"Batman"
"Rock"	"Pudge"	"Sunday Teddy"	"Knuckles"
"Boy Scout"	"Old Sarge"	"Wampum"	"Kid"
"Harold Growing Baines"	"Chief"	"Mr. Incredible"	"Shoeless Joe"
"Big Hurt"	"The Cuban Comet"	"Goose"	"Iron Pony"

White Sox Nicknames Challenge

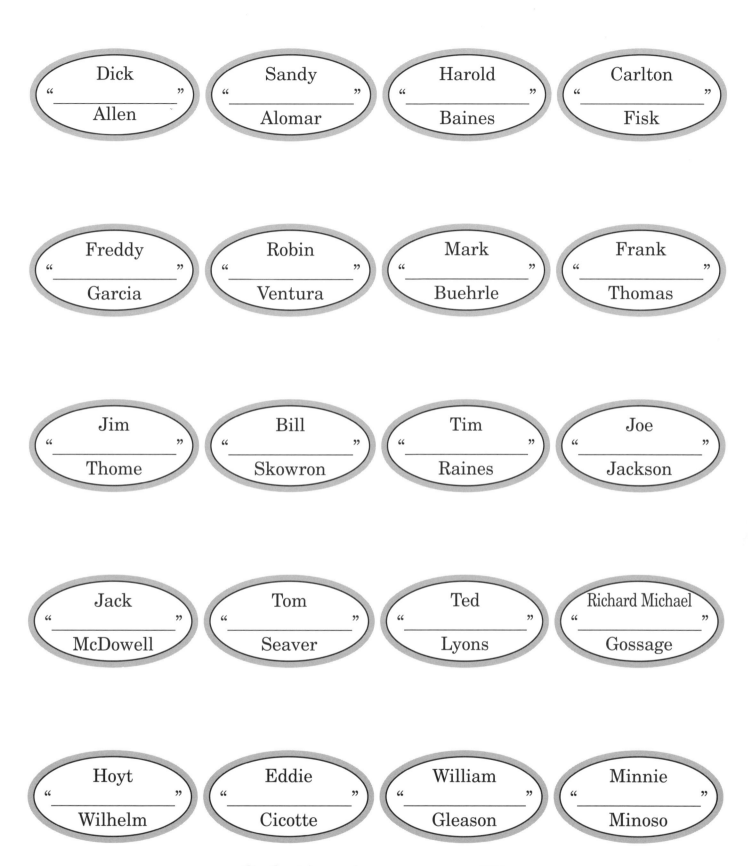

Dick "_____" Allen

Sandy "_____" Alomar

Harold "_____" Baines

Carlton "_____" Fisk

Freddy "_____" Garcia

Robin "_____" Ventura

Mark "_____" Buehrle

Frank "_____" Thomas

Jim "_____" Thome

Bill "_____" Skowron

Tim "_____" Raines

Joe "_____" Jackson

Jack "_____" McDowell

Tom "_____" Seaver

Ted "_____" Lyons

Richard Michael "_____" Gossage

Hoyt "_____" Wilhelm

Eddie "_____" Cicotte

William "_____" Gleason

Minnie "_____" Minoso

Solution is on page 55.

Use your knowledge about baseball terminology to solve the following crossword puzzle.

Crossword Puzzle 3 - Baseball Terminology

Across

3 Each year, the most outstanding pitcher from both the American League and National League wins this award.

5 Whenever David Ortiz clears the Green Monster wall, he's hit another _____. (two words)

6 When a pitcher gives up runs without his team committing an error, his _____ run average goes up.

7 When there's a runner on first, the second baseman and shortstop will try to turn a _____. (two words)

11 A slower pitch that starts at one side of the plate but finishes on the other is called a _____.

12 When the pitcher gives a batter first base rather than risk a home run, it's called an _____ walk.

16 Ted Williams is the last player to have one of these over .400. It's called batting _____.

18 A batter can score a runner on third without getting a hit. They just need to hit it deep into the outfield for a _____. (two words)

19 Lefties have a great one to first base. They'll try to catch the runner sleeping with their _____. (two words)

Down

1 You can hit a home run without clearing the fences, but you'd better be fast. This is called an _____ home run. (three words)

2 Nolan Ryan, Pedro Martinez, and Roger Clemens did this to many batters.

4 Carl Yastrzemski was the last player to accomplish this feat. He led the league in RBI, batting average, and home runs to win the _____. (two words)

8 When a pitcher starts his motion, then stops and tries to throw to first, he has committed a _____.

9 This is where the bench players sit during the game, or where the DH watches the game while his team is in the field.

10 This happens when a batter, instead of swinging, moves his hand up onto the barrel of the bat and tries to nudge the ball up one of the baselines.

13 Oops! When a grounder goes through the shortstop's legs or an outfielder muffs a fly ball, they get an _____.

14 Once you've reached first base, you can take a few steps toward second before the next pitch. This is called a _____.

15 Jonathan Papelbon, Bobby Jenks, and Mariano Rivera are experts at coming in at the end of the game to preserve the lead and record these.

17 This play is risky. When the manager sends the runner from third and the batter lays down a bunt, it's called a suicide _____.

Crossword Puzzle 3 - Baseball Terminology

Solution is on page 56.

Maze #1

Master the maze to help Mark Buehrle throw a strike to A.J. Pierzynski.

Solution is on page 56.

New addition Wilson Betemit displays his fielding skills for the fans.

Gavin Floyd's intense focus and flashes of brilliance have earned him a solid spot in the *White Sox* rotation.

Jermaine Dye's eyes never leave the ball as he stretches out, sacrificing his body to make the catch.

Word Search #2
Famous *White Sox* from the Past

```
W A M Y C P V E N T U R A H H W Z M N T
G P T R C S U G M Q K V L R L V S B B P
N P Q L A Z Y A M C M P L U E O I K A W
Z C S Z R O H S H Q D V E Z N V I Q I H
Y Q I L R U C S B H T O N P I F A L N M
U R S K A E Y O I Q W D W T I S V E E M
G U E M S F M G M L J F P E A E G V S Y
Z G K G Q I X R N V B Q R M L Y R M I H
O A Y L U S F E A I J E O I N L L C X N
D I D R E I L B L F L H L Y O N S H E E
G S C Y L O C A V W T P L T O V S L K Y
H E T I S C I F R B X Y P N T G L K J N
M H Z O R U W Q O B F O O A A I C C U Z
G U N O S A Y B C W W W F P U C K T G K
Q I T W E Z P R H H F Z Z G G C H J P W
M L I S B P Y A M P A P O A Q S T Y S X
```

Try to find all the words contained in the list below: (Hint: Words may be found by looking up and down, across, or diagonally. Some words are even spelled backwards!)

ALLEN	CARRASQUEL	FISK	KITTLE	PIERCE
APARICIO	DYKES	FOX	LYONS	SEAVER
APPLING	FABER	GOSSAGE	MCDOWELL	THOMAS
BAINES	FARMER	GUILLEN	MINOSO	VENTURA

Solution is on page 57.

Always willing to help the team, Brian Anderson sets for a bunt.

What's Different?

Find five differences between the two versions of the Chicago White Sox mascot shown below:

Solution is on page 57.

You Make the Call #2

Ball or strike? Fair or Foul? Safe or Out? Usually, the umpires have to make the tough decisions, but now... YOU MAKE THE CALL!

Here's the situation...

It's the top of the 8th inning at Progressive Field in Cleveland with Jermaine Dye on first base and Paul Konerko on third with one out. The score is tied at three. Sox catcher A.J. Pierzynski is at the plate and smacks a line drive to the left of Indians' second baseman Asdrubal Cabrera, who dives for the ball and deflects it off of Dye's helmet as he runs toward second base. The ball bounces from Dye's helmet into first baseman Ryan Garko's glove. Garko hesitates a moment, runs to tag first base, but does so moments after Pierzynski crosses it. Garko, believing he caught the ball legally and touched first base to put Dye out for the double play, rolls the ball to the mound and heads to the dugout with the rest of his teammates. Meanwhile, Konerko trots home and Dye runs quickly around the rest of the bases to score. (Keep in mind the ball remained in flight and did not touch the ground.)

What will the umpire rule?

Solution is on page 58.

An otherwise unemotional Mark Buehrle celebrates after completing a no-hitter on April 18, 2007.

White Sox Record Breakers
An Honors Quiz for Die-Hard Fans
Test Your *White Sox* Knowledge by entering the name of the player who holds the *White Sox* record below.

Most Home Runs in a Season

_____

Fewest Strike Outs in a Season

_____

Highest Batting Average in a Season

_____

Most Saves in a Season

_____

Most Complete Games in a Season

_____

Most Consecutive Scoreless Innings

_____

Most Triples in a Season

_____

Most Home Runs by a *White Sox* Player

_____

Most Games Played with the *White Sox*

_____

Most Stolen Bases by a *White Sox* Player

_____

Solution is on page 58.

Use your knowledge about the 2005 *World Series* Championship to solve the following crossword puzzle.

Crossword Puzzle 4 - 2005 *World Series* Championship

Across

3 This player struck out with 2 outs in the ninth inning of Game 2 of the ALCS, but was controversially awarded first base because the Angels catcher didn't field the pitch cleanly.

5 In the top of the 14th inning of Game 3 of the World Series, this player hit the winning home run.

9 This is the nickname of the Japanese second basemen that was a rookie sensation in 2005.

10 This fielder made brilliant plays for the final two outs of the World Series.

12 In the 2005 ALDS, the White Sox swept this team.

13 This player was named MVP of the ALCS.

14 This pitcher recorded 2 saves in the World Series.

15 The surprising ALCS Game 2 win was sealed through a run-scoring double by _____. (two words)

Down

1 This World Series MVP hit .438 during the World Series.

2 This Astros ace started Game 1 of the World Series, but had to leave early due to injury.

3 This outfielder is the first player in history to hit a home run in the World Series after not hitting any in the regular season.

4 This pitcher started Game 1 of every playoff series.

6 Game 3 of the World Series was the _____ game in World Series history, time-wise.

7 This pitcher got the save in the late-inning Game 3 World Series victory.

8 The only run in Game 4 of the World Series was scored by _____. (two words)

11 In the 6th inning of Game 3 of the ALDS, this pitcher came in with the bases loaded and no outs and didn't allow a run.

12 This hard-nosed outfielder was a fan favorite during the 2005 season.

Use your knowledge about the 2005 *World Series* Championship to solve the following crossword puzzle.

Crossword Puzzle 4 - 2005 *World Series* Championship

Solution is on page 58.

Diehard *White Sox* fan President Barack Obama threw out the first pitch in style before the second game of the 2005 ALCS.

Fiery *White Sox* manager Ozzie Guillen always has his head in the game.

Word Search #3
At the Ballpark

```
Q G K Z C Y M X M N G M J Q L J N S S D
O Z U E T E S N T A Y L S E M S U E H T
Y E I I T N E B C U I C O E R T R E I W
F D J U L P K E S J O U M Y C U V N E L
E R O L L R J L O O J G K O T O S I L U
O A C L P R T A R X R N U P C K L L D R
W O U J I R Y U H A D T L D S C A D S R
T B V L R A J D B V I U H K C A T E P Z
X E E H N Y K E Z H C N R G H L N R E S
R R P J I S C B R S Y O R K A B E T E M
V O Z H H Z E A S S W I S O B W M G D K
F C W I U T D U G E E U G T O I A F P U
T S T I F T N D R E T Y O H E M D L I Q
L H G J K S A I U C L I S P E P N I T A
K Q H L N Q F W P S J V U F T X U L C T
B Q G E Y J N E B R I C K S A W F P H F
```

Try to find all the words contained in the list below: (Hint: Words may be found by looking up and down, across, or diagonally. Some words are even spelled backwards!)

BLACK OUT	FUNDAMENTALS	SCOREBOARD
BRICKS	JERSEYS	SCULPTURES
BULLPEN	LEGACY	SHIELDS
DUGOUT	PETS	SHOWER
FAN DECK	RAIN ROOM	SPEED PITCH
FIREWORKS	RED LINE	SUITES

Solution is on page 59.

Maze #2

Master the maze to help Carlos Quentin send the ball to the fan in the upper deck!

Solution is on page 59.

Connect-the-Dots #2

Connect the dots to reveal this symbol of South Side pride.

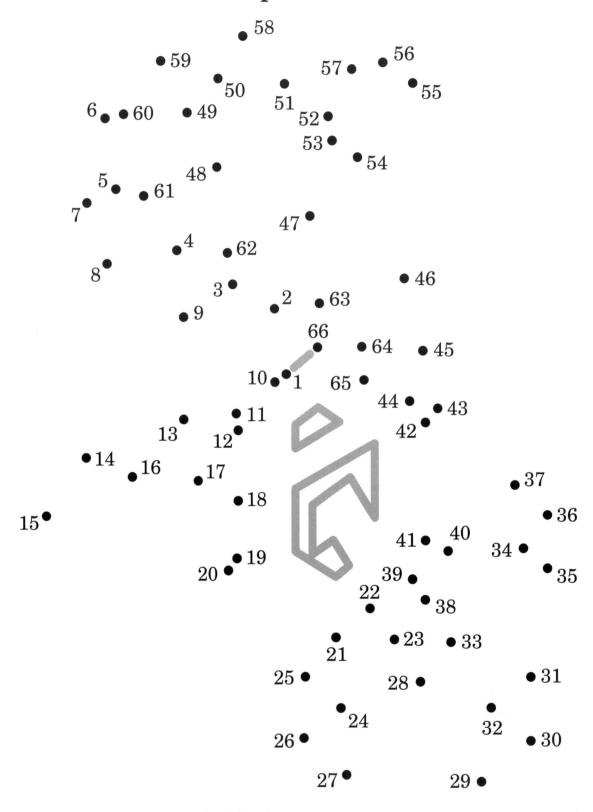

Mark Buehrle follows through on a well-placed change-up.

Slick-fielding Alexei Ramirez shows some finesse on a double play at second base.

Slugger Jermaine Dye trots around third base after blasting one into the seats.

White Sox Retired Numbers Game

Match the famous player or manager below with the retired number that they wore on the ball field. Enter the name of the player below the uniform containing their number on the next page.

Nellie Fox
- Played 14 seasons with the White Sox
- 12-time All Star
- Number retired in 1976

Harold Baines
- Played 3 stints with the White Sox
- 2nd in White Sox history in home runs
- Number retired in 1989

Luke Appling
- Played 20 seasons with the White Sox
- Entered the Hall of Fame in 1964
- Number retired in 1975

Minnie Minoso
- Played 12 seasons with the White Sox
- Named Rookie of the Year in 1951
- Number retired in 1983

Luis Aparicio
- Played 10 seasons with the White Sox
- 10-time All Star
- Number retired in 1984

Billy Pierce
- Played 13 seasons with the White Sox
- First Sox pitcher to start an MLB All-Star Game
- Number retired in 1987

Jackie Robinson
- In 1947, he was the first African-American to play in the Major Leagues
- Played for the Brooklyn Dodgers, 1947-56
- Number retired in 1997

Carlton Fisk
- Played 13 seasons with the White Sox
- Holds MLB record for games caught
- Number retired in 1997

White Sox Retired Numbers Game

9   _ _ _ _ _ _ _
     _ _ _ _ _ _ _

19   _ _ _ _ _
     _ _ _ _ _ _

4   _ _ _ _
     _ _ _ _ _ _ _ _

2   _ _ _ _ _ _ _
         _ _ _

11   _ _ _ _ _
     _ _ _ _ _ _ _ _ _

42   _ _ _ _ _ _
     _ _ _ _ _ _ _ _

3   _ _ _ _ _ _
     _ _ _ _ _ _

72   _ _ _ _ _ _ _
     _ _ _ _

Solution is on page 60.

Use your knowledge about *White Sox* history to solve the following crossword puzzle.

Crossword Puzzle 5 - *White Sox* Trivia

Across

3 Ozzie Guillen and Juan Uribe _____ to Nick Swisher's bat to get Swish out of his slump in 2008.

6 The Old _____ Sox logo, introduced in 1949, has been used longer than any other in franchise history.

7 Luke Appling led the American League in assists _____ seasons in a row.

11 The White Sox lost in the 2008 ALDS to the Tampa Bay _____.

13 The last White Sox strikeout champion was _____ in 2003 with 207 strike outs. (two words)

14 Rudy Karl _____ was the White Sox leadoff hitter when they won 99 games in 1983.

15 Number of White Sox outfielders inducted into the National Baseball Hall of Fame in the 20th century.

16 In 1917, the White Sox _____ 100 games, the most in franchise history.

17 The reason the White Stockings shortened their name to the White Sox was to fit _____ headlines.

19 The White Sox started the tradition of _____ in Hot Springs, AK.

Down

1 Tom Seaver set the Major League record for striking out ten _____ batters during a nine inning game.

2 Through 2007 the White Sox have beaten the _____ more than any other team in the American League (1,054 times).

3 Harold Baines played for the White Sox _____ separate times.

4 The White Sox were responsible for the last American League forfeit, due to Disco _____ Night in 1979.

5 In 2008, the White Sox led the Major Leagues in _____. (two words)

8 _____ was the last White Sox pitcher to both win and lose 20 games in a single season, 1973. (two words)

9 First White Sox Cy Young award winner was _____, in 1959.

10 The White Sox saw their highest _____ numbers in 2006 with 2,957,411.

12 Javier _____ was the starting pitcher on opening day in 2008.

18 _____ Rowland became the White Sox manager in 1915.

Use your knowledge about *White Sox* history to solve the following crossword puzzle.

Crossword Puzzle 5 - *White Sox* Trivia

Solution is on page 60.

DeWayne Wise calls off the other outfielders as he centers under the ball for the catch.

You Make the Call #3

Ball or strike? Fair or Foul? Safe or Out? Usually, the umpires have to make the tough decisions, but now... YOU MAKE THE CALL!

Here's the situation...

The Minnesota Twins are visiting U.S. Cellular Field. It's the bottom of the third inning and the game is tied at two. There are no outs and Alexei Ramirez is on first base with Brian Anderson at the plate. On a 3-2 pitch to Anderson, Ramirez is running. Anderson takes a low outside pitch for ball four. Not waiting for the umpire's call, Twins catcher, Joe Mauer, fires the ball to second base. Ramirez slides into the bag, beating the throw, but his momentum carries him past the bag. Twins second baseman, Alexi Casilla, tags Ramirez before he can return to the bag.

What will the umpire call?

Solution is on page 60.

The *Chicago White Sox* Mascot can often be found posing for pictures and dancing on the dugouts at U.S. Cellular Field.

Fill in the blanks

Learn more about Chicago

1. _____ Road divides Chicago's South Side from the North Side.

2. The South Side once was home to the Chicago _____.

3. _____ Place hosts the Chicago Auto Show each year.

4. Chicago's famous _____ Drive runs west of Soldier Field.

5. In 1892, the University of Chicago opened in Hyde Park along the _____ Plaisance.

6. _____ connects to the museum campus along Solidarity Drive.

7. Many of Chicago's museums are located on the South Side, including _____ Aquarium and The Field Museum of Natural History.

8. The Adler _____ and Astronomy Museum is currently the oldest in existence.

9. Chicago has been chosen as one of the final four candidates to host the 2016 _____ Olympics.

10. The Illinois Central Railroad opened its first _____ station at 51st and Lake Park Avenue in 1956.

Solution is on page 60.

Paul Konerko fires up the crowd after hitting his second home run of the game.

Solutions to Puzzles
Crossword Puzzle 1, page 5
White Sox History

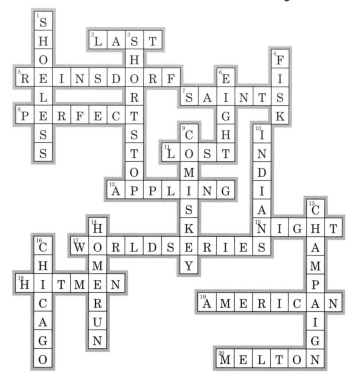

Solution to Word Search #1, page 9:
White Sox Players

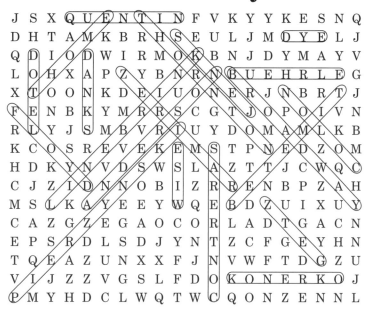

Try to find all the words contained in the list below: (Hint: Words may be found by looking up and down, across, or diagonally. Some words are even spelled backwards!)

ANDERSON	COLON	DYE	KONERKO	RAMIREZ
BETEMIT	CONTRERAS	FLOYD	LINEBRINK	THOME
BROADWAY	DANKS	GETZ	PIERZYNSKI	THORNTON
BUEHRLE	DOTEL	JENKS	QUENTIN	WISE

Solution to *White Sox* Player Challenge, page 11

1. A.J. Pierzynski
2. Bobby Jenks
3. Jim Thome
4. Carlos Quentin
5. Mark Buehrle
6. Paul Konerko

7. Jermaine Dye
8. John Danks
9. Alexei Ramirez
10. Brian Anderson
11. Scott Linebrink

Solution to Crossword Puzzle 2, page 13
White Sox Fun Facts

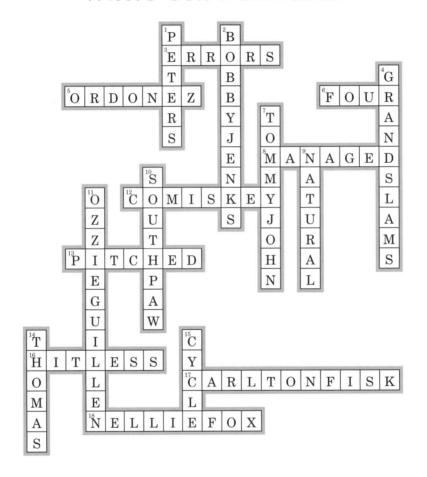

Solution to You Make the Call #1, page 17

Ramirez will have to return to second base since the ball is dead once in the stands. Thome is out.

Solution to solve the *White Sox* Scramble, page 18

1. COMISKEY PARK

2. FRANK THOMAS

5. SMALL BALL

6. OZZIE GUILLEN

3. SOUTHPAW

4. FIREWORKS

7. SOUTH SIDE

8. AMERICAN LEAGUE

Solution to solve the *White Sox* Nicknames, page 21

Dick *"Wampum"* Allen

Sandy *"Iron Pony"* Alomar

Harold *"Harold Growing Baines"* Baines

Carlton *"Pudge"* Fisk

Freddy *"Chief"* Garcia

Robin *"Batman"* Ventura

Mark *"Burls"* Buehrle

Frank *"Big Hurt"* Thomas

Jim *"Mr. Incredible"* Thome

Bill *"Moose"* Skowron

Tim *"Rock"* Raines

Joe *"Shoeless Joe"* Jackson

Jack *"Black Jack"* McDowell

Tom *"Boy Scout"* Seaver

Ted *"Sunday Teddy"* Lyons

Richard Michael *"Goose"* Gossage

Hoyt *"Old Sarge"* Wilhelm

Eddie *"Knuckles"* Cicotte

William *"Kid"* Gleason

Minnie *"The Cuban Comet"* Minoso

Solution to Crossword Puzzle 3, page 23
Baseball Terminology

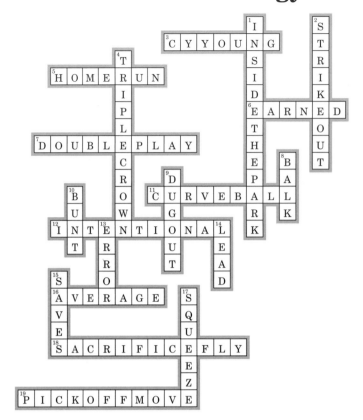

Solution to Maze 1, page 24

Solution to Word Search #2, page 28
Famous *White Sox* from the Past

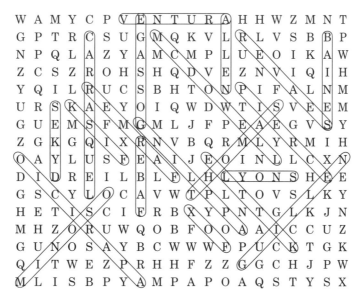

Try to find all the words contained in the list below: (Hint: Words may be found by looking up and down, across, or diagonally. Some words are even spelled backwards!)

ALLEN	CARRASQUEL	FISK	KITTLE	PIERCE
APARICIO	DYKES	FOX	LYONS	SEAVER
APPLING	FABER	GOSSAGE	MCDOWELL	THOMAS
BAINES	FARMER	GUILLEN	MINOSO	VENTURA

What's Different? page 30

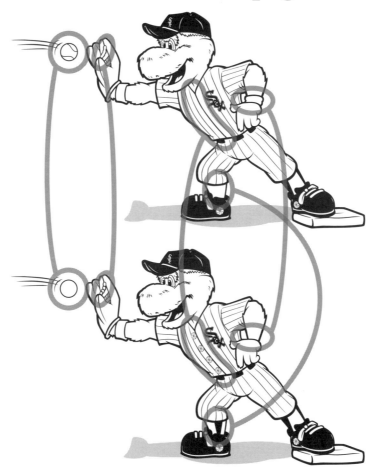

Solution to You Make the Call #2, page 31

It is not a legal catch. The ball is in play. Two runs score and the inning continues with the White Sox leading 5-3 with one out. Pierzynski remains on first since he did not run once he saw the Indians leave the field.

Solution to *White Sox* Record Breakers, page 33

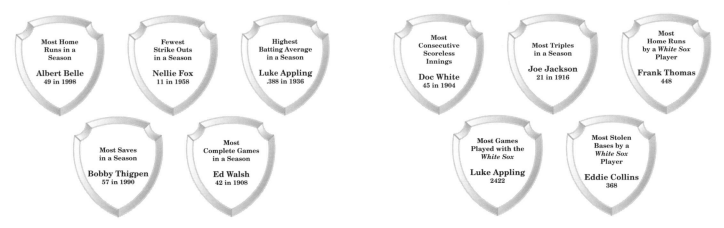

Most Home Runs in a Season
Albert Belle
49 in 1998

Fewest Strike Outs in a Season
Nellie Fox
11 in 1958

Highest Batting Average in a Season
Luke Appling
.388 in 1936

Most Saves in a Season
Bobby Thigpen
57 in 1990

Most Complete Games in a Season
Ed Walsh
42 in 1908

Most Consecutive Scoreless Innings
Doc White
45 in 1904

Most Triples in a Season
Joe Jackson
21 in 1916

Most Home Runs by a *White Sox* Player
Frank Thomas
448

Most Games Played with the *White Sox*
Luke Appling
2422

Most Stolen Bases by a *White Sox* Player
Eddie Collins
368

Solution to Crossword Puzzle 4, page 35
2005 World Series Champions

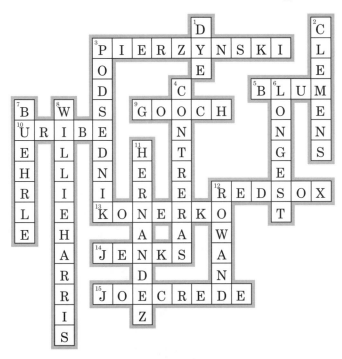

Solution to Word Search #3, page 38
At the Ballpark

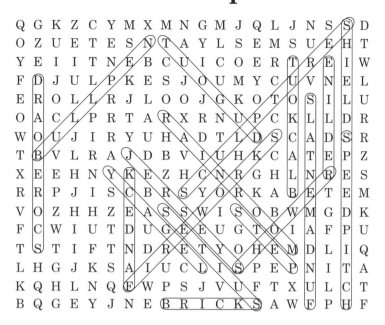

```
Q G K Z C Y M X M N G M J Q L J N S S D
O Z U E T E S N T A Y L S E M S U E H T
Y E I I T N E B C U I C O E R T R E I W
F D J U L P K E S J O U M Y C U V N E L
E R O L L R J L O O J G K O T O S I L U
O A C L P R T A R X R N U P C K L L D R
W O U J I R Y U H A D T L D S C A D S R
T B V L R A J D B V I U H K C A T E P Z
X E E H N Y K E Z H C N R G H L N R E S
R R P J I S C B R S Y O R K A B E T E M
V O Z H H Z E A S S W I S O B W M G D K
F C W I U T D U G E E U G T O I A F P U
T S T I F T N D R E T Y O H E M D L I A
L H G J K S A I U C L I S P E P N I T A
K Q H L N Q F W P S J V U F T X U L C T
B Q G E Y J N E B R I C K S A W F P H F
```

Try to find all the words contained in the list below: (Hint: Words may be found by looking up and down, across, or diagonally. Some words are even spelled backwards!)

BLACK OUT	FUNDAMENTALS	SCOREBOARD
BRICKS	JERSEYS	SCULPTURES
BULLPEN	LEGACY	SHIELDS
DUGOUT	PETS	SHOWER
FAN DECK	RAIN ROOM	SPEED PITCH
FIREWORKS	RED LINE	SUITES

Solution to Maze #2, page 39

White Sox Retired Numbers Game, page 45

9 Minnie Minoso   **19** Billy Pierce   **4** Luke Appling

2 Nellie Fox   **11** Luis Aparicio

42 Jackie Robinson   **3** Harold Baines   **72** Carlton Fisk

Solution to Crossword Puzzle 5, page 47
White Sox Trivia

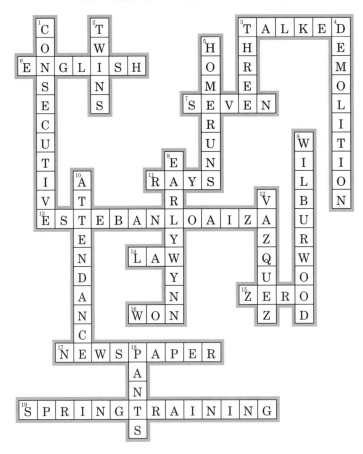

Solution to You Make the Call #3, page 49

Ramirez is out, even though it was ball four to Anderson. If Ramirez had not initially touched second base, he would have been safe. Also, if he had not been running, he would have been able to take second base once ball four was called.

Solution to Fill in the blanks, page 51

1. Roosevelt   3. McCormick   5. Midway   7. Shedd   9. Summer
2. Cardinals   4. Lake Shore   6. Northerly Island   8. Planetarium   10. Hyde Park

We hope that you enjoyed the first edition of the
Chicago White Sox Coloring and Activity Book!

Please contact us with questions or comments at:

Hawk's Nest Publishing LLC
84 Library Street
Mystic, CT 06355
www.HawksNestPublishing.com

Books for the Young and Young at Heart...

To order additional copies of this book:

Phone

Pathway Book Service
800-345-6665 or 603-357-0236

Web

www.WhiteSoxColoringBook.com

Mail

Hawk's Nest Publishing
c/o Pathway Book Service
P.O. Box 89
Gilsum, NH 03448

Hawk's Nest Publishing, LLC

Books for the Young and Young at Heart...

HawksNestPublishing.com